This book belongs to

....

....

A catalogue record for this book is available from the British Library
Published by Ladybird Books Ltd.
A Penguin Company
80 Strand, London, WC2R 0RL, England
Penguin Books Australia Ltd, 250 Camberwell Road,
Camberwell, Victoria 3124, Australia
New York, Canada, India, New Zealand, South Africa

001 - 10 9 8 7 6 5 4 3 2 1

© Eric Hill, 2004
This edition published 2011
Eric Hill has asserted his moral rights under the
Copyright, Designs and Patents Act of 1988
All rights reserved
Planned and produced by Ventura Publishing Ltd
80 Strand, London WC2R 0RL

ISBN 978-0-72326-755-3

Printed in China

Spot's
Garden

Eric Hill

One sunny day, Spot was helping
Grandpa in the garden.
"This is so much fun, Grandpa,"
Spot said. "I think I'd like to
have my own bit of garden to
grow things."

6

"That's a good idea, Spot," said Grandpa. "You can have the patch by the fence. It's nice and sunny." "Thank you, Grandpa!" said Spot.

"You'll need something to plant in your garden," said Grandpa. So he and Spot went to the shop to buy seeds.

"There are so many colourful seed packets," said Spot. "I can't decide which to choose." "Carrots and lettuce are good to grow," said Grandpa. "And they taste delicious in salads."

Grandpa showed Spot how to dig
out rows for planting.
"The lettuces can go on one side,
and the carrots on the other,"
said Grandpa.

Spot made his rows nice and straight.

Then it was time to plant the seeds. Grandpa showed Spot how to sow the seeds in the rows they had dug.

"Tweet! Tweet!" called some birds, as they flew down from the tree. "I think the birds want to help us, Grandpa," said Spot.

"I think the birds want to help themselves – to the seeds!" laughed Grandpa. "We'd better make a scarecrow to keep them away."
With some wood from the shed, and an old shirt, Grandpa and Spot made a scarecrow.
"The scarecrow can have my hat," said Spot.

The next day, Spot went to water his vegetable garden.

"Grandpa," he said, "I don't think the scarecrow is working!"
"Oh, dear!" said Grandpa.

"Why don't we give the birds some seeds of their own?" said Spot. "Then they won't need to eat mine."

"That's a very good idea, Spot," said Grandpa. "I've got some sunflower seeds in the shed. Birds love sunflower seeds!"

Spot helped Grandpa fill a tray with sunflower seeds and put them out on a little table. The birds seemed to like them much more than Spot's vegetable seeds!

"Let's give the birds some water, too," said Spot, "in case all those sunflower seeds make them thirsty."

Spot watered his vegetable garden every day. He carefully pulled out the weeds, too.

Sometimes Steve and Helen came to help. Soon Spot's vegetables began to grow!

The plants in Spot's garden grew and grew. At last the lettuces were ready for picking.
"But where are the carrots?" Spot asked Grandpa.

"Right here," said Grandpa,
"waiting for you." He showed
Spot how to loosen the soil and
tug at the carrot tops.
Up came the carrots!

"Look!" said Spot. "There's something else in my garden. How did they get here?"

"The birds must have dropped
some of the seeds we gave them,"
said Grandpa, "and they grew
into these lovely sunflowers."

Spot invited Steve and Helen to come for a picnic lunch. Grandpa made a salad with the lettuce and carrots from the garden.
"Thank you all for helping me with my garden," said Spot.

"And thank you for sharing your vegetables," said Steve and Helen.
"Tweet! Tweet!" said the birds.
"I think they're saying thank you, too!" laughed Grandpa.